To my wife, Ragan, and my children, Abby, Ben, and Molly—
I want to be like you all when I grow up.

All rights reserved. Published in the United States by Random House Children's Books, a division of Random House, Inc., New York.

Random House and the colophon are registered trademarks of Random House, Inc.

Visit us on the Web! www.randomhouse.com/kids

Educators and librarians, for a variety of teaching tools, visit us at www.randomhouse.com/teachers

Library of Congress Cataloging-in-Publication Data
Jessell, Tim.
Falcon / by Tim Jessell. — 1st ed.
p. cm.
ISBN 978-0-375-86866-5 (trade) — ISBN 978-0-375-96866-2 (lib. bdg.)
[1. Imagination—Fiction. 2. Falcons—Fiction. 3. Birds—Fiction. 4. Flight—Fiction.] I. Title.
PZ7.J55316Fal 2012
[E]—dc22
2011012758

MANUFACTURED IN CHINA

10 9 8 7 6 5 4 3 2 1

First Edition

FALCON

TIM JESSELL

RANDOM HOUSE 🏠 NEW YORK

If I were a falcon . . .

I would ride
the north wind
to faraway
places.

With the sound
of tearing paper,
my wings would
slice through
the air.

No bird would dare
to venture out when
I came into view,
for my eyes would
be as strong as my
talons were sharp.

I would fly along
the coastline and
over the sea, darting
above the waves
and scattering
seabirds before me.

Then up, up, up
the sea winds
would lift me,
high above
the cliffs.

If my wings
grew tired,
I would find
shelter among
the rocks and
fall asleep to
the sound of
the crashing
surf.

. . . I came to
the man-made
cliffs of a great
booming city.

There, I would
take my perch,
while far below me
pigeons cooed and
flapped and fluttered
in the shadows.

I would stand,
calm above
the noise and
the crowds,
and then . . .

Wings tucked tight,

I would dive

down, down,

down.

The sidewalks would rush up at me. The people would gasp.

At the last minute,
I would open
my wings, and
my speed would
carry me up.

The sidewalks would rush up at me. The people would gasp.

At the last minute,
I would open
my wings, and
my speed would
carry me up.

The sound of
surprised laughter
would fade fast
as I returned to
my perch. I might
just do that again.

Oh, if only I were a falcon . . .